Dear Parents:

Congratulations! Your child is taking the first steps on an exciting journey. The destination? Independent reading!

STEP INTO READING® will help your child get there. The program offers five steps to reading success. Each step includes fun stories and colorful art or photographs. In addition to original fiction and books with favorite characters, there are Step into Reading Non-Fiction Readers, Phonics Readers and Boxed Sets, Sticker Readers, and Comic Readers—a complete literacy program with something to interest every child.

Learning to Read, Step by Step!

Ready to Read   Preschool–Kindergarten
• big type and easy words • rhyme and rhythm • picture clues
For children who know the alphabet and are eager to begin reading.

Reading with Help   Preschool–Grade 1
• basic vocabulary • short sentences • simple stories
For children who recognize familiar words and sound out new words with help.

Reading on Your Own   Grades 1–3
• engaging characters • easy-to-follow plots • popular topics
For children who are ready to read on their own.

Reading Paragraphs   Grades 2–3
• challenging vocabulary • short paragraphs • exciting stories
For newly independent readers who read simple sentences with confidence.

Ready for Chapters   Grades 2–4
• chapters • longer paragraphs • full-color art
For children who want to take the plunge into chapter books but still like colorful pictures.

STEP INTO READING® is designed to give every child a successful reading experience. The grade levels are only guides; children will progress through the steps at their own speed, developing confidence in their reading. The F&P Text Level on the back cover serves as another tool to help you choose the right book for your child.

Remember, a lifetime love of reading starts with a single step!

*For Mom and Dad, whose gift of a puppy dog filled
my childhood with everlasting friendship*
—H.J.

To Appa, with love!
—G.L.

How to say the words in this book:
Bindi: BIN-dee
Burfees: BURF-fees
Diwali: dih-VAA-lee
Diyas: DEE-yas
Katlis: KUHT-lees
Laddoos: LUH-doos
Prasaad: pruh-SAAD
Rangoli: rung-GO-lee

Text copyright © 2024 by Harshita Jerath
Cover art and interior illustrations copyright © 2024 by Geeta Ladi

All rights reserved. Published in the United States by Random House Children's Books, a division of Penguin Random House LLC, New York.

Step into Reading, Random House, and the Random House colophon are registered trademarks of Penguin Random House LLC.

Visit us on the Web!
StepIntoReading.com
rhcbooks.com

Educators and librarians, for a variety of teaching tools, visit us at RHTeachersLibrarians.com

Library of Congress Cataloging-in-Publication Data is available upon request.
ISBN 978-0-593-70675-6 (trade) — ISBN 978-0-593-70676-3 (lib. bdg.) —
ISBN 978-0-593-70677-0 (ebook)

Printed in the United States of America
10 9 8 7 6 5 4 3 2 1
First Edition

This book has been officially leveled by using the F&P Text Level Gradient™ Leveling System.

A Sweet Diwali

by Harshita Jerath
illustrated by Geeta Ladi

Random House 🏠 New York

This is Raina.
She lives
with her family.

This is Lion.

Lion is Raina's dog.

Lion is small.
But he feels big.
WOOF!

His bark is loud
like a roar.
His walk is proud
like a king.

Raina and Lion are
best pals.

They walk.

They play.

They snuggle.

Today is Diwali.

Diwali is
a festival of lights.

It is a reminder
to choose
light over darkness.

Raina dresses up
for Diwali.

Her dress sparkles.

Her bindi shines.

She puts sparkles
on Lion's collar.
Now he is ready, too!

Raina draws a design
on the floor.
She fills it
with colorful sand.

"Cool rangoli!" says Dev.

He is Raina's brother.

Next they light
clay lamps
called diyas.
The lamps light up
the house.

Lion loves
the glowing lights.

The scent of sweets
fills the house.
There are
diamond katlis
and square burfees.

There are
round laddoos
for Lion, too!

The family offers
prayers.
Papa rings
the worship bell.

Mummy gives
the sacred sweet.
It is called prasaad.

Fireworks light up
the dark sky of Diwali.
BOOM! POP!

Lion does not like
loud noises.

He hides under the bed.

Raina wants to help.
She offers Lion
an oat laddoo.
Yum!

She also puts
doggy earmuffs
on him.
This helps a lot.

The family eats
dinner.
It is a sweet
and savory feast.

But Lion just wants
more laddoos!

He eats three.

He eats four.

He eats five.

Uh-oh!

Now Lion does not
feel well.

Raina sees
that Lion ate too much.

She carries him to bed.

She reads him a story.

Soon he feels better.

Lion loves Raina.

And Raina loves Lion.